Christmas 1994

To my dearest and best
friend Elaine,

I know you will
enjoy these special Christmas

Twelve Tales of Christmas

stories. My favorite is,
"Blessed Be the Poor"

May Heavenly Father
bless you c̄ his choicest blessings
always.

With eternal love,

Kathy

Twelve Tales of Christmas

Richard M. Siddoway

BOOKCRAFT
Salt Lake City, Utah

Library of Congress Catalog Card Number: 92-72662
ISBN 0-88494-845-5

Second Printing, 1993

Printed in the United States of America

Contents

Preface

Every Christmas is different. It is not so much that Christmas changes, but that we change. My earliest Christmas remembrances seem silly when viewed half a century later. My latest remembrances would be viewed as somewhat stilted and sober by someone much younger.

Early Christmas memories are dominated by Santa Claus and gifts received. Later ones are dominated by Jesus Christ and gifts given.

While each of these stories is based on actual people and events, each has been altered to some extent. Sometimes this has been to preserve the anonymity of those involved. Sometimes events have been combined to make a better story. The intent has not been to deceive but to entertain.

The final story is reported from several conversations with people who knew the two girls on whom Amy's character is based.

This book is arranged chronologically. Therefore, it begins with the very silly and ends with more sober thoughts. Such is life.

1

I'm a Believer

I spent the first six years of my life living in my grandfather's house. I don't suppose that's too unusual, but most of my cousins also lived there. My grandfather believed a "family that stays together, stays together." So when he built his house he built it with that philosophy in mind.

The first floor of the house contained a living room, dining room, kitchen and pantry, master bedroom, library, and bathroom. The second floor had been divided into six small apartments, each with a bedroom, sitting room, and bathroom. My grandfather expected his children to marry and move their spouses into the apartments they had occupied while growing up in his house. Surprisingly, most of his children did just that. To this day, fifty years after my birth, I call my parents by their first names, since I heard a multitude of aunts and uncles address them that way during the formative years of my life.

It was a great experience. With all of my cousins growing up in the same house, we never lacked a playmate. It also led to memories of Christmas that were, to say the least, unusual.

Behind the kitchen and pantry on the first floor of our home was a screened-in sitting porch. Since air conditioning had not yet been invented, this screened-in porch provided a place to sit on a summer's eve, be protected from bugs, and yet take advantage of any cooling breezes. On the second floor was a similar room built above the sitting porch. It was called the sleeping porch.

The sleeping porch was about ten feet wide and as long as the house was wide, about forty feet. During the winter months the screened windows were covered with insulated panels, and the sleeping porch became a playroom for all of the children in the house.

Every family has developed its own set of legends about Christmas. At our home Santa Claus decorated the Christmas tree. The morning of Christmas Eve a large piñon pine was pushed, pulled, and forced through the front door into the corner of the living room. The ceiling was ten feet high and the tree always brushed it. A delicious aroma filled the house. Once the tree was placed in its stand, there was considerable discussion, adjusting, and turning before the tree was finally secured. Piñons are really not shaped like traditional Christmas trees. There are always bare spots where a branch should have grown but didn't. When the tree was brought into the house it was supposed to "come down." This is a non-faith-promoting experience in which non-existent branches are supposed to relax in the warmth of the house and magically droop into place, filling the bare spots on the tree. . . . But the aroma was marvelous.

During the afternoon, all of the grandchildren who were old enough to not wet the bed pulled their mattresses onto the sleeping porch. Pillows, sheets, and down-filled quilts, called "down puffs," were arranged for the night.

Dinner was over by seven. The tree stood undecorated, still waiting to "come down," in the corner of the living room. Stockings, many stockings, were hung from the mantel. Children were tucked into bed on the sleeping porch. Then two different events began simultaneously.

Downstairs the adult members of the family began decorating the Christmas tree. Upstairs we began a night-long party. My grandfather had a large wind-up alarm clock. It had been wound and put in a place of honor near the doorway that led from the sleeping porch to the upper hall. The down puffs were arranged over chairs to form a tent. Inside the snug warmth of the tent the older cousins took turns reading stories to us by flashlight. We had begun spending our allowances on flashlight batteries since Halloween and had built up a stockpile to make it through the night.

I do not believe there is one word mentioned about Santa Claus in *The Wizard of Oz*, but it will always be a Christmas story to me, since we read it from cover to cover under our sleeping porch tent on Christmas Eve. The reading was interrupted on a regular basis by one or another of us asking, "What time is it?" It was generally one or two minutes later than the last time the question was asked. The night wore on.

Downstairs the adults had finished decorating the tree. Our living room was large enough that each child had a specific location for gifts. The presents were wrapped and in place. Then began the events that made these Christmases so memorable.

The fireplace in the living room was enormous. As a five-year-old child I could walk into the fireplace without having to stoop. The chimney was about three feet square. It had been equipped with a metal ladder, similar to a fire escape, to allow a chimney sweep to work in the chimney. Uncle John Santa Claus climbed carefully into the chimney.

Above the sleeping porch, in the attic, was an exercise room my uncles had built. There were weights, a chinning bar, and other pieces of equipment. Two or three of my uncles would climb the steep stairway to the attic, tiptoe to the end of the attic above the sleeping porch, and suddenly begin tapping around on the wooden floor, at the same time jingling sleigh bells. In the tent on the sleeping porch there was instant panic. Another Christmas legend at our house was that if Santa found you awake when he arrived, he wouldn't leave any gifts.

Instantly down puffs were pulled from chairs, the tent collapsed, order was restored, and children began snoring softly. My mother would open the door from the hallway. "Children, Santa's here. Would you like to see him?"

We stretched and yawned and pretended to be waking up. Our house had two staircases, one just inside the front door, the other from the hallway between pantry and kitchen. It was down this back stairway we crept. Quietly we filed into the dining room. Between the dining room and living room were French doors. These multi-paned doors were rigged

4

with a counterweight system so that by turning a handle the door slid open. According to Christmas legend, if you looked through these glass doors and made no sound, you were invisible to Santa Claus. We lined up, noses pressed against the French doors.

Our attention was focused on the fireplace. In fact, we were so intent that we failed to notice that the tree had been decorated and gifts were arranged all over the room. Suddenly Santa Claus dropped into the fireplace. He brushed the soot from his clothes, reached down, and plugged in the tree lights. As if by magic the tree was decorated. This always brought a gasp of joy from one or more of us children. Santa heard the gasp, turned toward the French doors, saw us children, and started to leave.

We were horrified! We still had not noticed the gifts in the living room. We were watching Santa Claus too intently to notice anything else. My mother or one of my aunts would open the French doors, rush into the living room, and plead with Santa Claus. "We were the ones who awakened the children. They were asleep." Our heads all nodded agreement.

At last Santa would agree to leave gifts and talk to each child. A big black leather chair was pushed into the center of the room. Santa sat in the chair, and each child in turn sat on his lap. This Santa Claus was amazing! He knew each of us by name. He knew each of us by deed and misdeed. He extracted promises of good behavior and told us we had to sleep until seven o'clock before coming down to open gifts. Then, looking around the room one last time, he walked over to the mantel, stooped over and entered the fireplace, placed his finger aside his nose, nodded, stood up, and rose into the chimney.

We raced up the back stairs to the sleeping porch. Overhead we heard Santa's reindeer and sleigh bells as he flew off to the next housetop. Had there been windows in the sleeping porch, we'd have seen him fly away.

The rest of the night dragged on. Every minute or two one of us would ask what time it was. The reading by flashlight continued. We drifted into sleep and out of it until seven o'clock. Then we raced down to the living room to open gifts.

It strikes me singularly that I cannot remember one of the gifts I received. I can remember exactly, however, the feelings of excitement and love produced by this unique Christmas experience. These, of course, are numbered among the most important gifts of all, and explain why I love the Christmas season so much.

2

The White Snows of Winter

The winter before my eighth birthday stands out in my mind for two reasons. First, my cousin Bill had come to live with us for a while; second, the snow was so deep one Friday that the schools closed. Actually, there is a third reason why I remember that winter, and it involves the first two.

My cousin Bill had been living with his parents in the Washington, D.C., area during World War II. When the war ended, my uncle decided to move his law practice to the Salt Lake area. He purchased a building lot and contracted to have a house built. When it was time for school to begin, the house was not yet finished. Bill came to live with our family so he would not have to transfer schools in the middle of a school year.

We lived on Roosevelt Avenue. Ages ago Lake Bonneville filled the Salt Lake Valley. We lived on the steep slope that had plunged from the ancient beach into the lake. My next-door neighbor Allen had a marvelous sleigh-riding hill in his backyard. Allen's place had a great deal going for it. There were horse chestnut trees in the front yard, apple trees in the backyard, and a little fish pond fed by a spring that flowed right out of the side of the hill.

As Christmas approached, our attention turned toward what Santa Claus would bring us. Since the snow had begun falling early that winter, my heart had turned toward a sled. Not any sled, but a Flexible Flyer, the Rolls Royce of sleds. One afternoon Allen, Bill, and I were walking home from Emerson Elementary School, and the subject of Christmas presents came up.

"I want a Flexible Flyer!" I exclaimed.

"Me, too," chimed Allen. Our imaginations swooped as we stomped homeward through the snow.

Bill, even at the age of nine, was a master of one-upmanship. He remained strangely quiet for a block or two, then suddenly said, "I don't want a Flexible Flyer. They're for little kids. I want skis."

My seven-year-old brain crunched to a halt. Skis! I had never personally seen anyone on skis. My only experience with skiing was in watching the sports portion of newsreels which preceded movies. These films seemed to focus on either ski jumping or inglorious falls. Skis! Bill smugly led us home in silence.

During dinner Bill slyly brought up the subjects of Santa Claus and Christmas gifts. My father asked me what I wanted Santa Claus to bring me.

"A Flexible Flyer!"

My father's eyebrows raised.

"What do you want, Bill?" my mother asked.

"I thought I might ask him for some skis."

My father dropped his fork. "Skis? You'll break your leg. Those things are dangerous. You're not going to catch me on two little barrel staves sliding down a mountain. No sir!"

I looked at Bill's face. There was no sign of disappointment. "I just didn't want to ask for anything as expensive as a Flexible Flyer. Skis cost a lot less."

My father's face relaxed. "I guess," he said, "it depends on how they're used, whether they're dangerous or not." Bill knew at that moment the skis were his.

Christmas morning dawned cloudy and cold. There was already eight or ten inches of snow on the hill behind Allen's house, and the clouds threatened to add to the accumulation. Bill and I dashed down the stairs and into the living room. There, under the Christmas tree, was my Flexible Flyer. Its polished wood glowed in the lights of the Christmas tree. The red runners gleamed. I could hardly wait to get dressed and try it out. "Bill, look!" I said, pulling the sled out from under the tree.

Bill stood transfixed. Sticking out from his side of the tree was a pair of skis. They were not the fiberglass, machine mass-produced skis of today; these were made of wood. A slot was cut through each ski from side to side, and a leather strap, like a small belt, went through the slot. These skis had no fancy bindings to entangle and frustrate a nine-year-old. You merely stood on the ski and cinched the strap across your foot. In a flash Bill had the skis out from under the tree and was strapping his bare feet onto the skis. His face glowed. In his mind he was racing down the highest peaks of Switzerland.

"Let's get dressed! Let's go!" he whooped as he

pulled his feet from the straps and ran for the stairway to our bedroom. We quickly dressed and pulled our snowsuits on over our clothing. The bane of our existence was our galoshes. After your feet were stuffed into them, you had to force a half dozen little metal tongues through slotted clasps and close them. This often meant peeling your thumbnail backward while trying to force the clasps closed. Finally dressed, I grabbed my sled, Bill his skis, and out of the door we clomped.

The hill behind Allen's house had already attracted a crowd. Several of my friends, Allen, Ladd, and Neil, had all asked for Flexible Flyers for Christmas. Santa Claus had delivered. The three of them were sliding down the hill when Bill and I arrived. Clutching my sled, I carried it up the hill. Bill followed with his skis thrown over his shoulder.

Allen's hill was fairly steep. The slope ran about 150 feet and then flattened out until you ran into the fence between Allen's house and ours. Our two driveways paralleled each other along the fence line. Just to the east of Allen's driveway was the four-by-six-foot fish pond. On either side of the fish pond were large apple trees. It was a pristine setting, white with snow.

Allen's hill was deceptive, however. As you climbed it, the length apparently increased. From the top, at least to my seven-year-old mind, the slope was endless. We readied ourselves for the first run down the hill. Bill stood, skis over his shoulder, surveying the slope. Suddenly he turned to me. "Where's the rope on your sled?"

The handlebars of my Flexible Flyer had been drilled so a rope could be attached. In my excitement to go sleigh riding, I had forgotten to put a rope on my sled. "You can't pull your sled up the hill without a rope," Bill said. Of course I had dragged my sled up the hill already, but Bill ignored that fact. "I'll take it down and put a rope on it for you." Bill propped his skis against the fence, took my sled from me, and rode it down the hill.

I stood in the cold and watched my friends glide down the hill on their sleds. After some time Bill reappeared around the corner of Allen's house. He pulled my sled to the bottom of the hill, dropped the rope, and trudged up the hill. "There. Your sled has a rope."

I slipped and slid down the hill to my sled, grabbed the rope in my mittened hand, and dragged my Flexible Flyer to the top of the hill. When I arrived at the top Bill was inspecting his skis. As I reached him he said, "I notice your sled drags a little. Have you sanded the paint off the runners?" I wrestled the sled to its back. The runners were still bright red. "You can't go really fast with paint on your runners. I'll go get some sandpaper." And with that Bill turned my sled over and rode it down the hill.

A few minutes passed before Bill reappeared with a piece of sandpaper clutched in one mittened hand, the rope to my sled in the other. When he reached the bottom of the hill, Bill dropped the rope to the sled and climbed up to me with the sandpaper. "Now you can sand your runners." Bill handed me the sandpaper. I clomped down the hill in my galoshes, turned the sled over, and began sanding the paint from the runners. It took quite a bit of time to get most of the paint off. Bill still had not come down the hill on his skis.

I dragged the sled to the top of the hill. "Did you put wax on your runners? If you don't they'll rust, and the wax makes you go faster." I shook my head. "I'll go get some," offered Bill. He took the rope from my hand and slid on down the hill on my sled.

A few minutes later Bill dragged the sled around the corner of Allen's house and pulled it to the bottom of the hill. He climbed up the hill and handed me a stick of foul-smelling wax. "Ski wax," he said, "the best kind." Down the hill I clomped, turned my sled over, and began trying to apply wax to the runners. At last I dragged my sled up the hill.

"When you gonna ski down the hill?" Allen asked Bill. "I think you're afraid!"

"I'm not afraid," spat out Bill. "I'm just waiting for you guys to pack the snow with your dumb little sleds."

"Bill's a scaredy-cat! Bill's a scaredy-cat!" chanted Allen. Within seconds the rest of the gang had picked up the chant. Finally Allen said, "If you're not scared, let's see you go down the hill."

I was just finishing putting a little more wax on my runners at about the same time Bill strapped on his skis. While Bill stood quaking at the top of the slope, I finally turned my sled over and started my first ride down the hill. Whether Bill launched himself or Allen pushed him has been a point of debate for many years. Whatever the case, Bill let out a scream and began to slide down the hill. His arms windmilled. He struggled to keep his balance. He screamed even louder.

I had picked up considerable speed when I heard Bill's screams through my stocking-capped ears. I turned and looked over my shoulder. Bill was on a collision course with my sled. Still looking over my shoulder at the wildly gesticulating Bill, I swerved to avoid being hit by him. Crash! I hit an apple tree with my left handlebar and hand. My screams were louder than Bill's.

Bill either wisely sat on the back of his skis or fell over. At any rate, he came to a stop just shy of going into the fish pond. He kicked off his skis and came back to me. I was lying on the ground screaming. The left handlebar had broken. So had my wrist.

Bill told me to lie on my sled and he would pull me home. I tried to run home instead, but Bill grabbed me and forced me to lie down on my sled. He grabbed the rope, which now was attached only to the right handlebar and to a broken piece of wood that used to be the left handlebar. As he began to pull me, the sled turned over and dumped me onto my injured left arm. I ran home.

The doctor, who was not happy about having his Christmas morning disturbed, swathed my arm in forty pounds of plaster and hung it from a sling around my neck. I returned home and inspected my sled. Most of the left handlebar had shattered. The sled was ruined! My Flexible Flyer had died!

"Well," Bill mused, "I wouldn't worry too much. By the time you get your cast off, there probably won't be any snow left anyway." Thus ended Christmas Day, 1947.

3

Roses Are
Red

Today is December 23. It is on this day each year that I do penance for an act I committed in 1947, when I was seven years old. I was in the third grade at Emerson School and had been blessed with a marvelous teacher named Miss Heacock. She was not much taller than I, and had dark red hair and smiling green eyes. I credit her with any love I have for classical music, because she spent part of every Thursday morning introducing us to the lives of the great composers and playing recordings of music by Beethoven, Brahms, Bach, and other great musicians. I loved school because of the influence of this wonderful woman.

As Christmas approached we made decorations for our schoolroom. Miles of red and green paper strips were pasted into interlocking loops to form paper chains as we listened to Handel's *Messiah*.

Pictures of Santa Claus were drawn and painted with water colors. Stained-glass windows were approximated as Miss Heacock ironed our crayon drawings between pieces of scrap paper. A Christmas tree was placed in one front corner of the room, and the odor of pine replaced the particularly pungent aroma of oil that arose from the decades-old hardwood floors of our classroom. It was then that Miss Heacock announced we were to have a Christmas party on the day we were released for Christmas vacation. We were all excited.

Fate had blessed us with a peculiar situation that year. There were exactly as many girls as boys in our class. Miss Heacock decided, perhaps in an attempt to introduce us to the social graces, that each of us would purchase a gift for another student in the room. Each boy would supply a gift for a girl and vice versa. The gifts were to cost no more than twenty-five cents. There have been moments in my life when I have known exactly what was going to happen. I claim no great gift of prophecy, but, nevertheless, I have known. As Miss Heacock began walking down the aisles, a box of boys' names in one hand, one with girls' names in the other, I knew the name I'd draw would be Violet's.

Violet was a sorry little girl who had been placed in our class that year. She was very plain and did little to help her looks. Her hair was rarely combed, she wore the same dress every day, and, worst of all, she wet the bed and rarely bathed. Violet sat in the back corner of the room, partially because she chose to sit there, but also because the rest of us had moved away from her. When the room warmed up, the aroma of Violet mixed with the perfume of floor oil and became almost overpowering. Seven- and eight-year-old children can be cruel, very cruel. Violet had been the target of most of our cruelty during the school year.

Miss Heacock approached my desk with the box of girls' names. I reached into the box, shuffled the names around, and finally withdrew the folded scrap of paper. I placed it before me on my desk. My fingers trembled as I unfolded it. There it was, as I knew it would be: "Violet." I quickly wadded up the paper and shoved it into my pants pocket. The bell rang for recess.

"Who'd you get?" asked my best friend, Allen.

I panicked. I couldn't let anyone know I'd gotten Violet. "We're supposed to keep it secret."

"Sure, but you can tell *me*," Allen probed. "I'll tell you who I got. Just between us, okay?"

"Miss Heacock said to keep it secret." My voice squeaked a little.

Suddenly Allen smiled. Earlier in the year I had made the mistake of telling him I thought one of the girls in our class, Margo of the honey-colored hair, was pretty. I had endured considerable abuse since that disclosure. "I'll bet you got Margo's name. That's why you won't tell. You got Margo!" Immediately he was running around the playground shouting that I'd gotten Margo's name. So much for Allen's ability to keep a secret.

I slunk back into the school, face aflame. The rest of that Friday crawled by. Finally the last bell rang. As I was pulling on my galoshes I felt a hand on my shoulder. "Is something wrong?" I looked up into Miss Heacock's emerald eyes. "You seemed awfully quiet this afternoon."

"I'm okay," I stammered. My mind had been struggling with the Violet problem all afternoon. I had reached a possible solution; I wouldn't get Violet anything. Since we were maintaining secrecy, no one would know. "Maybe," I said, "I won't be able to get a present. My father makes me earn all my spending money," I lied, "and I might not have a quarter to buy a present."

A look of concern came over Miss Heacock's face. "If you can't afford a quarter, I'll give you one. It will be our little secret."

I trudged home through the snow. No other brilliant escapes from the situation entered my mind. Christmas was the following Thursday, and the party would be on Tuesday. I had only three days to find a way out of my misery. Perhaps I could become sick, but that path was fraught with peril, since my mother made us stay in bed all day when we were sick, and I might be in bed Christmas Day if she suspected I was really not sick. At last I reached home.

The house smelled wonderful. I could tell my mother had been baking bread. I hurried to the kitchen in hopes of melting gobs of butter on a slice of warm bread. My mother greeted me. "Miss Heacock phoned. I'm sure your father and I can come up with a quarter for a Christmas present." My heart sank into my galoshes. Now there was no way out.

Saturday morning it was snowing. My mother exulted about a white Christmas while I pulled on my snowsuit and galoshes and prepared for the four-block trek to the Economy Drug Store. My mother gave me a quarter and a dime "just in case" and sent me off to do my Christmas shopping. I took time to investigate everything along the way, prolonging the inevitable as long as possible.

Since the previous evening, I had been contemplating what to buy for Violet. Nothing seemed really appropriate. As I wandered up and down the aisles of the Economy Drug, galoshes squeaking mournfully, I discovered my choices were somewhat narrowed by the twenty-five-cent limit. I considered purchasing five nickel candy bars but discarded that idea, since Violet probably liked candy bars. As I reached the end of the counter, I saw the gift, and a terrible plan exploded full-blown in my mind. Not only did I see the gift, but I knew how I would present it to Violet. There on the shelf were small, crown-shaped bottles of cologne. I selected one from the display and twisted off the lid. Years later when I read novels that used the phrase "she reeked of cheap perfume," my mind always flashed back to the first whiff of cologne from that bottle in the Economy Drug. It had only one redeeming feature. It cost a quarter.

I sloshed back home with my purchase. Thankfully, my mother did not sniff the cologne. She merely commented on how lovely the little bottle was. She helped me find a box and wrap my gift. I went to my room, found a pencil and paper, and wrote the following poem:

> *Roses are red,*
> *Violets are blue,*
> *Put this stuff on*
> *So we can stand you.*

I did not sign it. I sealed it in an envelope and taped it to the gift.

Monday morning I left for school earlier than usual. When I arrived I went to my classroom. The door was open, but Miss Heacock was not in her room. Quickly and furtively I placed the gift under the Christmas tree. So far so good.

By the time the school bell rang, Miss Heacock was playing Christmas carols on the phonograph, and more and more gifts were being placed under the tree. We became more excited about tomorrow's Christmas party as the day wore on. Miss Heacock carefully looked at each gift and checked off names in her roll book.

On Tuesday our party was preceded by a semi-annual desk clean out. At last all of the papers had been removed, crayon boxes lined up neatly, and pencils sharpened and put away. It was time for the party!

We drank punch from paper cups and ate cookies and candy canes, and then it was time to distribute gifts. As we sat in our seats Miss Heacock selected a present from beneath the tree and called out, "Sandra." Sandra, somewhat embarrassed, walked to the front of the room and took her present back to her desk. She was unsure whether she should open it or not. "You may open it, Sandra," said Miss Heacock.

Several more presents were distributed before Miss Heacock called out, "Violet." Violet walked slowly to the front of the room. Miss Heacock extended her hand and delivered my gift. Violet, eyes glistening, walked back to her seat. I shifted in my seat so I could see her reaction. She placed the unopened gift on her desk and opened the envelope. Suddenly she began to quiver; a tear formed in the corner of her eye and ran down her cheek. Violet began to sob. She grabbed her present and ran from the room. Miss Heacock, reaching for a gift, did not see her go.

The enormity of what I had done sank home. Tears filled my eyes. There have been moments in my life when I wished I could back up ten minutes and correct errors I had made. This was one of those moments. I am sure my name was eventually called. I am sure I was given a gift. I remember nothing of this. I merely wallowed in guilt. Finally the party ended, and I walked home.

As Christmas vacation came to an end I began to realize I would have to face Violet when I went back to school. Even though I had not signed my name, I was certain she had figured out who had written that terrible poem. How could I face her? But like it or not, school began again. It began without Violet. Her seat was empty. It was empty the next day and the next. Violet had moved.

Twelve years passed. I entered a classroom at the University of Utah and took my seat. The professor began to call the roll. "Violet," he called. The girl in the seat directly behind mine answered, "Here." My blood ran cold. As discreetly as possible I turned and looked at her. She had matured, she had changed from an ugly duckling into a swan, but there was no doubt it was Violet.

When class ended I turned to her. "Violet," I said, "I don't know if you remember me. We were in the same class in third grade at Emerson School."

She looked at me, and her forehead wrinkled. "I'm sorry, I really don't remember your name. I was only in that class for part of the year."

"Violet, may I take you to lunch? I need to ask your forgiveness."

"For what?" She looked puzzled.

"I'll tell you at lunch, okay?"

We walked silently to the Union Building, through the cafeteria line, and to a table. "What do you need to talk to me about?"

"How much do you remember about our third grade class?" I asked.

"The music," she answered. "Our teacher played such beautiful music. I think she's the reason I'm a music minor today.

"It had been such a tough year for my family. My father died that July, and we found a little house to rent. It was so crowded with six children. I had to sleep with my two little sisters, and they both wet the bed. I can remember how embarrassed I was to come to school smelling so bad, but the bathtub didn't work, and we had to wash out of a washtub after heating the water on our coal stove. Usually there wasn't time to bathe in the morning." The words were tumbling out as Violet remembered bitterly that third grade experience. "I used to come to school and hide in the back corner."

I was finding it harder and harder to confess. As Violet spoke, the coals were heaped higher and higher upon my head. At last she was silent. "Violet, do you remember the Christmas party?"

Tears formed in her eyes. "Oh, yes."

"Violet, can you ever forgive me? I was the one who wrote that terrible poem that sent you sobbing from the room."

She looked puzzled. "What poem? I was crying because I hadn't had a quarter to buy a gift and yet someone had given a gift to me. I couldn't stand the guilt and the shame."

"Violet, there was a card attached to your gift. On it I wrote a terrible poem. Don't you remember?"

Violet tipped her head back and laughed. "I couldn't read in the third grade. I don't think I even looked at your poem." Then the knife twisted. "What did it say?"

"Violet, it doesn't matter. Just forgive me, please."

"Come on, what was the poem?"

I chose not to compound my guilt with a lie, so I quoted it to her.

"It seems appropriate to me," she laughed. "I forgive you."

We finished lunch, and I walked out of the Union Building with a lighter heart. However, every December 23, I still do penance for the cruelty of youth.

4

Pins and Needles

Bill, my cousin, blamed my mother. It really wasn't her fault, but Bill had trouble accepting blame. I will admit my mother had supplied the safety pins, but only to help us keep from losing our mittens. Perhaps I should begin at the start.

When the first snow fell in the winter of 1948, my mother bought Bill and me each a pair of mittens. Mittens were what little kids wore. I was eight and Bill was ten, far beyond the mitten stage. We wanted gloves. Mittens had two major problems. First, the heat from your hands melted the snow and soaked your hands in cold water. Second, when you tried to form a snowball, little pieces of snow stuck to the wool fibers until your palm was covered with clots of snow that stuck to the snowball you were trying to form. We hated mittens. Within two days of receiving our new mittens we had managed to leave them at school.

Schools have lost-and-found boxes. I suspect our mittens joined thousands of unclaimed articles, some dating back to before the Civil War.

My mother tired of buying new mittens for Bill and me, so she devised a plan to help us keep from losing our mittens. She took each of our coats and threaded a piece of string up the left arm and down the right arm. She tied a safety pin on each end of the string and pinned the string to our mittens. This was not a thrilling prospect for us. Not only were mittens for little kids, having them attached to a string with safety pins was for *very* little kids. Whenever we left the house, Bill unsnapped his mittens from the safety pins and crammed them into his coat pockets.

As Christmas approached we began the arduous task of gift shopping. The Economy Drug Store was only four blocks from our house. This drugstore had an amazing assortment of inexpensive gifts. It was a prime spot for Christmas shopping for Bill and me with our limited resources. Friday morning, Christmas Eve, we climbed the hill to the drugstore. Bill and I received ten cents allowance each week. We had been saving for Christmas for several weeks, and Bill suggested we pool our money and give joint gifts. I contributed the seventy cents I had saved, Bill contributed his thirty cents, and together we planned how to spend a whole dollar.

As soon as we left the house Bill unsnapped the safety pins and stuffed his mittens into his coat pockets. Although the snow was falling lightly and it was cold, Bill refused to wear his mittens. He thrust his hands into his corduroy pants pockets as we clomped up the hill. Walking in corduroys reminded me of listening to crickets. With every step the legs chirped as they rubbed against each other. "Well," said Bill, "let's figure out how many presents we have to buy."

Bill and I had discussed Christmas presents every night since Thanksgiving. I had a little sister and brother. Bill was an only child, and his parents were living in Washington, D.C. We had agreed to get my sister and brother a present and, if money permitted, buy a gift for my mother and father.

"Let's see," pondered Bill, "we need to get Bobsy and John something, then maybe your Mom and Dad, and . . ." Lightning struck. "Holy cow, we forgot each other!" I could see our already thin resources being stretched beyond their limits. "John's only three, maybe he won't notice if we don't get him something," suggested Bill.

"He'll notice," I muttered. "Bill, we've gotta get John and Bobsy presents. Maybe there won't be enough money to get each other anything, but we gotta get them presents."

We scuffled on silently up the hill to the Economy Drug. This drugstore would be small by today's supermarket/drugstore standards, but it was sufficiently large for us in 1948. As we entered the front door there were three aisles stretching out ahead of us. Each of the counters had a Christmas display arranged at the end of it. We began walking down the aisles looking at the wide selection of possible gifts. My sister, Bobsy, was five. We selected a small cardboard box with three little paper envelopes of bubble bath. The bubble bath had exotic names like Gardenia and Tropic Flower. Inside the envelope was a barely soluble powder, which, if placed in the bathtub under the tap and the water turned on full force, produced an inch or two of bubbles. However, when you climbed into the bathtub you felt as if you were sitting in a pile of sand. But the most important thing about it was that it cost only twenty-five cents. "It's perfect for Bobsy," I said, and clutched a box of the bubble bath.

Selecting a gift for John, who was only three, was a little more difficult. Bill favored a comic book, which cost a dime, but I wasn't sure. "He doesn't know how to read."

"We could read it to him," said Bill, "I'll bet he'd really like it." At that moment I spied a display of small balsa wood gliders and diverted Bill's attention to them. There were basically two models. One was about ten inches long and was just a glider. It consisted of the fuselage of the plane, a wing that was pushed through a slot in the fuselage, and a tail rudder and stabilizer that fit in the rear of the plane. It cost a dime. The second model had a propeller and a long rubber band to give it powered flight. It cost a quarter. "Let's get John a glider," Bill exclaimed. I reached for the twenty-five cent model. "He won't be able to wind the propeller," said Bill. "Get him the plain glider." I plucked a cellophane-wrapped glider from the display.

"Let's see," calculated Bill, "we still have . . . uh . . . sixty-five cents left. Why don't we split the money and go look for a present for each other."

"Bill, we still have my Mom and Dad." Bill shrugged his shoulders. Suddenly he turned and reached for a box of kitchen matches.

"Let's get them these matches. They're always looking for matches to light the stove. They'd really like 'em, and they only cost a dime." Before I could react, Bill had handed me the matches to carry along with the bubble bath and glider. It was true we were always looking for matches to light the old coal stove in our kitchen. Maybe it wasn't such a bad idea after all.

"Let's see, now we have . . . uh . . . how much?" Bill struggled with the arithmetic. "Oh yeah, fifty-five cents. Let's be fair about it. I'll take a quarter to buy you a present and you can have thirty cents to buy me one." Bill took the quarter and turned down the aisle. Looking back over his shoulder, he said, "And I don't want any of that junky bubble bath."

I began exploring the shelves in search of the proper gift for a ten-year-old. I looked at a box of toy soldiers, but Bill wasn't much of a toy soldier fan. Similarly I passed over a rubber ball and a little web bag of marbles. Chinese checkers were out of the question. Then I spied the perfect present for Bill—a putt-putt boat. When you placed a putt-putt boat in the water, a small amount of water flowed into a little boiler about the size of a quarter. Beneath the boiler was a spot for a small flat candle. When the candle was lighted it heated the water in the boiler until it boiled and the steam exploded out through two tiny tubes which protruded from the stern, underwater. The boat was thrust forward with a putt-putt sound. Bill would love one. There was only one problem. They cost thirty-nine cents.

I considered my options. I could replace John's glider and hope he really was too small to notice. But I knew that wouldn't work. Finally I called out to Bill, "I need another dime." Bill appeared from around the end of the counter.

"You need a dime? All I've got is a quarter." Actually, all we had between us was four quarters. My mother had traded us quarters for our dimes so we wouldn't have as many coins to lose.

"Give me the quarter," I said, "and I'll go pay for our presents, then I'll give you the change."

"I'll come pay with you," grinned Bill.

"Then you'd see what I'm getting you. Don't you want it to be a surprise?"

Bill looked hurt, but finally handed me the quarter. He retreated to the back of the store while I picked out his putt-putt boat and added it to the other three gifts. Quickly I walked to the front of the Economy Drug and placed my gifts on the counter. Mr. Johnson, the owner, smiled at me. Then he glanced around, "Where's your cousin?"

"He's in the back. I don't want him to see what I'm getting him." I pointed at the putt-putt boat.

Mr. Johnson rang up the purchases. "That's eighty-four cents and eight mills for the governor."

I had forgotten tax. We had little plastic tokens to pay sales tax. They were colored grey, green, blue, and orange. We played tiddlywinks with them. Mr. Johnson took my four quarters and handed back fifteen cents and two ten-mill plastic tokens. My gifts were placed in a paper bag. I rolled over the top of the bag so Bill couldn't peek.

"Bill," I called out, "I've got your money." Immediately Bill appeared from behind the first counter. I handed him the fifteen cents.

"Now you go to the back of the store while I pay for your present," he said. "And no peeking."

Mr. Johnson interrupted, "Why don't you leave your sack here on the counter while you go to the back of the store. I'll watch it for you." Obediently I placed my sack of treasures upon the counter. I walked to the back of the drugstore.

A moment or two passed before Bill called from the front counter, "Let's go." I started for the front of the store. Mr. Johnson handed me my paper bag with a look of relief on his face, and we turned to go. What happened next left this Christmas impressed indelibly in my mind.

At the end of the first counter was a small decorated Christmas tree. Artificial ones had not yet been invented, so this tree was a small fir stuck in a pail of sand. A strand of lights had been wired securely to its branches, and hanging on the tree were a number of pairs of gloves—gloves, not mittens. As we turned to go, the safety pin hanging from the left sleeve of Bill's coat caught the string of lights on the Christmas tree. The right safety pin embedded itself in Bill's coat. The next step he took brought the Christmas display, tree and all, crashing to the floor. I let out a scream. Bill joined the chorus. Mr. Johnson muttered. All three of us descended on the tree and tried to repair the damage. The sand from the bucket had spilled on the wooden floor. Without it the bucket was not heavy enough to support the tree, so when we set the tree upright, it fell over again. I began scooping sand up with my hands. Bill helped pick up gloves and get them out of the sand and broken light bulbs. Mr. Johnson muttered.

At length Mr. Johnson retrieved a dust pan and a whisk broom. We swept up the sand and refilled the pail. The tree was jammed back into the sand and the broken bulbs replaced.

"I'm sorry," said Bill. "It was an accident. We didn't mean to do nothing like this."

"Get out," begged Mr. Johnson. I began to sniffle. Bill picked up our sacks, handed mine to me, and we walked out of the Economy Drug.

The next morning, Christmas morning, I gave Bill a putt-putt boat. Bill gave me a pair of gloves to match his new ones.

Unfortunately my mother knew every piece of clothing we owned. Since the gloves did not appear on her inventory, we were forced to return them. Bill did let me play with his putt-putt boat.

5

Let Us Have Christmas the Whole Year Round

It had been two weeks since I began working as a clerk-typist at the police department, and payday was here. My sophomore year at the university began in about six weeks and tuition loomed before me. Suddenly, as I stood filing arrest records, I noticed that everyone else had disappeared from the records and identification department. I looked at the service counter and saw a little, elderly woman. I went to the counter. "May I help you?"

Although it was a warm late summer day, she was dressed in a black frock coat, which reached almost to her heels. On her head was a hat that looked very much like half a cabbage. Her fingers were wrapped with pieces of adhesive tape. She carried a black cardboard suitcase in each hand. In response to my question she looked at me with watery eyes above heavily rouged cheeks, hoisted the suitcases to the counter, and pointed at her ear with one bandaged finger. Apparently she was deaf.

Slowly, majestically, she opened one battle-scarred suitcase. She removed a rectangle of cardboard from inside. Draped over it were about a dozen neckties, arranged side by side on display. As I peered into the suitcase, I could see another ten or twelve pieces of cardboard, each draped with ties. There was a cardboard display of red ties, blue ties, green ties, striped ties, polka-dotted ties, every kind of tie I could imagine. As I looked through the selection, she opened the other suitcase and revealed more ties.

At length I selected a plain navy blue tie, which met uniform specifications. "How much?" She studied my lips, a crease on her brow, then smiled. She held up one finger. "They cost a dollar?" I queried. She nodded her head.

I took a dollar bill from my wallet. From beneath the piles of ties, my little saleslady removed a piece of tissue paper and a cardboard tie form. She draped my tie over the cardboard form, tenderly wrapped it in tissue paper, and taped it with cellophane tape. She took the dollar I proffered and handed me the tie. Wistfully she gazed around the records bureau, and seeing no one else, closed her suitcases, turned, and walked out of the door.

As if by magic, people reappeared. "Who was that?" I asked.

"Lily the Tie Lady," the shift sergeant replied. "She comes every payday to sell you her one-dollar ties. We've all learned to find other things to do when she comes. You will too."

But I didn't. I couldn't turn my back on this pitiful little creature who regular as clockwork showed up every payday. For the next two and a half years I pur-

chased a tie twice a month. At Christmastime I purchased ties for gifts. Always the routine was the
same. The tie was draped over a cardboard form,
wrapped in tissue paper, and exchanged for the dollar bill. And Lily never changed. She was always
dressed in her too-long coat and half-cabbage hat.
Her fingers were always wrapped with tape. Regard-
less of the season, Lily remained the same.

One Christmas our shift sergeant, Ed, in a burst of
Christmas spirit, bought a tie from Lily and gave her
a twenty-dollar bill. "Keep the change," he said. "Buy
yourself a Christmas present." Lily shook her head in
a vigorous no. But Ed persisted and refused to take
change. Lily wrapped his tie and left.

The next day Ed reported, "You remember I gave
Lily twenty dollars yesterday? When I unwrapped
the tie I bought from her, there was a twenty-dollar
bill wrapped with it."

I thought of Lily as being immortal. But one payday she failed to appear. A few days later the local
papers carried her obituary and her story. Lily had
been the widow of a very wealthy man. When he
died she had been approached by many charities asking for donations. Lily wondered how much of that
money really reached the people she intended to
help. At that moment she conceived a wonderful
plan. She would go to the people themselves and give
them a gift.

After some investigation Lily decided that most
public employees were underpaid. She also realized
that most of them were required, either by uniform or
convention, to wear ties. So Lily began purchasing
neckties. Some were imported, some were domestic,
but all cost much more than a dollar. Lily developed
her costume, the black frock coat and cabbage hat,

and covered her carefully manicured fingers with bandages. The ties were placed in two old cardboard suitcases. Her chauffeur loaded the suitcases in her limousine and drove her to alleys near the police department, the fire department, and municipal offices. Lily carefully emerged from the back alleys as Lily the Tie Lady.

Every time I purchased a tie from Lily I thought I was doing her a favor. Little did I realize she was giving me a gift in return.

Lily the Tie Lady, I salute you. You truly knew how to keep Christmas, the whole year round.

6

A Christmas Found

Why Sergeant Olson decided to take his Christmas holiday on Christmas Eve instead of Christmas Day I'll never know. But I am eternally grateful to him for doing so, for on that Christmas Eve an event transpired that made the Christmas of 1960 memorable to me.

The Salt Lake City Police Department at that time occupied a building on the southeast corner of State Street and First South, where the Federal Building now sits. You entered from State Street into a long, white-tiled hallway. At the far end of the hall sat the desk sergeant's desk.

I normally worked in the records and identification department, but because Sergeant Olson had taken his Christmas holiday a day early, this Christmas Eve I found myself sitting at the desk. It was a slow night, as you would expect. Salt Lake had been blanketed with snow, and gentle, large flakes continued to fall. The night was cold.

About 9:00 P.M. the front doors opened and a young black man entered the police station. He was fairly tall, an inch or two over six feet, and dressed poorly for the winter season. His faded jeans had holes in the knees. His thin jacket barely covered his worn T-shirt. He had crossed his arms and placed his hands in his arm pits to keep them warm. He walked quickly down the white-tiled floor to the desk.

"Can I help you?"

He reached into his back pants pocket and pulled out a thin, well-worn wallet. "I found this up the street," he indicated, jerking his head north up State Street.

I took the old black wallet from his hand, opened it, and examined the contents. There was an identification card, three photographs, and twelve ten-dollar bills. I looked at the photographs. One was a very old wedding picture, frayed around the edges. The other two were pictures of a young man, one in a graduation cap and gown, the other in military uniform.

The identification card indicated that the wallet belonged to Joseph Allred. I knew the address. It was an inexpensive hotel-rooming house complex a couple of blocks away from the police station. "Let me try to call Mr. Allred," I said, "and then I can get some information from you for the report."

The phone rang six or seven times before a frail woman's voice quietly said, "Hello."

I explained who I was and that a wallet belonging to Joseph Allred had been found and turned in. I heard a gasp over the phone. Then, "Oh, thank you, thank you."

I asked if they would like to come to the station to pick up the wallet.

"We'll be right down."

I hung up the phone and turned to the young man who had returned the wallet. I told him the Allreds were coming down to pick it up. "I'd better be on my way, then," he said, turning. "I don't want them trying to give me a reward." And he started toward the door.

"Just a minute," I called after him. "I need to have some information for my report." He turned slowly back to the desk.

"Name?"

"Charles Johnson."

"Address?"

"I'm a student at the University of Utah. I live in the dorms." He told me which residence hall and his room number.

I could tell from his accent that Charles Johnson had not been born and raised in Utah. "What brings you to Utah?"

"I got a scholarship."

For the next few minutes I learned about Charles Johnson. He was the eldest of eleven children and had been born and raised in a rural community in the Deep South. His mother and father ran a small farm. He had done well in school and had been offered a scholarship at the University of Utah. He was a junior student. At Christmastime the last two years he had earned enough money to take the bus back home for the holidays, but this year the cost of going to school had increased and the wages of his part-time job had not. He couldn't afford to go home for Christmas. This Christmas Eve he had taken the bus downtown from campus and was walking the streets, looking in store windows, trying to get the Christmas spirit. Tomorrow he would telephone home for Christmas. He had seen the wallet in the snow as he walked down State Street. Here he was.

As I finished filling out the report, the front doors opened and through them came an elderly couple. Neither was over five feet tall. They clutched each other tightly as they shuffled down the hallway toward the desk. Whisps of the woman's spun sugar hair stuck out from beneath an ancient bandanna. Her old cloth coat had been mended in several places. Snowflakes sparkled from her eyebrows as she removed her glasses and wiped the moisture from them with a torn handkerchief.

The man removed his hand to reveal an almost-polished bald head with a tiny fringe of white hair. He had wrapped a scarf around his neck above the mottled gray overcoat. At last they reached the desk. The old man extended his cold, bony hand. "I am Joseph Allred. This is my dear wife, Mary."

"Mr. Allred, I am pleased to return your wallet to you. Would you please check the contents to see if anything is missing."

Mary Allred replaced her thick spectacles and looked over the contents of the wallet with her husband. They first looked at the pictures. "We were married over fifty years ago," she said, inspecting the worn wedding picture. Pointing at the pictures of the young man, she said, "This was our son. We were so proud of him. The war was a terrible thing."

Joseph Allred counted out the bills. "It's all here! Our rent money and our food money. It's all here!"

After the excitement died down, the Allreds wanted to know who had found the wallet. During their interrogation Charles sat quietly listening and watching. I turned to him. "Let me introduce you to Charles Johnson. He's a student at the university. He found your wallet."

As Charles stood to meet the Allreds, Mary shuffled forward and wrapped her arms around him. Her face barely reached his chest. "God bless you, my son."

Joseph extracted one of the ten-dollar bills and reached toward Charles. "Your reward. I wish it could be more."

"No, no," said Charles. "I can't take your money."

"You're not from around here, are you?" asked Mary.

Charles admitted he was not.

"Why aren't you going home for Christmas?"

"I can't afford it," was the straightforward reply.

The two elderly people looked at each other for a moment, and then Joseph spoke. "Please, come with us. Share our Christmas. Let it be our gift to you. Please."

"But I have no gift for you."

"You are our gift," said Mary. "He—our Joshua— he was your age."

The three of them turned and walked toward the door. Two small, white-haired elves, one on each side of the tall black man, who that Christmas found room in the inn.

7

The Least of These

We married in August and settled into a small apartment near the university where both of us went to school. We each had a year until graduation and scrimped and struggled through the autumn quarter. Now Christmas was approaching and we had little money between us to squander on Christmas gifts. We managed to put aside enough money for winter-quarter tuition and books, and that had taken all we had except for rent, utilities, and food.

We walked through the department stores of Salt Lake arm in arm with the confidence of better days ahead. My bride paused before a winter coat, caressing it with her eyes and fingers. Together we looked at the price tag—seventy-five dollars. Tuition for a quarter was eighty-five dollars. We both knew the coat was out of the question. Her old coat, seam-split and stained, would have to do another year. But

Christmas is a time for dreaming and hoping, and her gaze lingered long upon the coat.

When I received my paycheck on December 20, we paid what bills we owed and discovered we had twenty dollars left for Christmas. Together we found a Christmas tree lot where a stack of broken branches lay. For fifty cents they let us fill the trunk of our old car with pine boughs. We drove home and wired them together into the semblance of a Christmas tree. With a borrowed string of lights and some handmade ornaments, we created our first Christmas tree.

We agreed to spend no more than five dollars apiece in shopping for each other. While my wife drove the car to do her shopping, I walked the half dozen blocks to the Grand Central drugstore to see how far I could stretch five dollars. After considerable searching I selected a paperback novel my wife had commented about and a small box of candy. Together they came to $4.75. As I approached the checkout stand, I was met with a long line of shoppers, each trying to pay as quickly as possible and get on with the bustle of the season. No one was smiling.

I waited perhaps half an hour, and only three people were ahead of me in the line when I became aware that the line had ground to a halt. The clerk was having an animated discussion with an elderly customer. He was tall and thin, with an enormous shock of white hair that had been carefully parted and combed. He was wearing a pair of navy blue slacks that ended nearly three inches above his shoes. His plaid shirt was missing a button, and the sleeves of the shirt protruded two or three inches past the sleeves of his light jacket. He had an ancient leather wallet in his hand.

"Sir," barked the clerk, "the price of insulin has

gone up. I'm sorry, but we have no control over that. You need four more dollars."

"But it has been the same price ever since my wife started taking it. I have no more money. She needs the medication." The man's neck was turning red and he was obviously uncomfortable with the situation. "I must have the insulin. I must."

The clerk shook her head. "I'm sorry, sir, but I have no control over the prices. You need four more dollars."

The woman immediately ahead of me in line began to mutter under her breath. She had other purchases to make and resented this clot in the artery of Christmas shopping. "Hurry up, hurry up," she whispered loudly.

"Please let me take the insulin and I will bring you back the four dollars," pleaded our elderly friend. The clerk was adamant; he had to pay before he got the medicine.

The man standing behind him put a hand on his shoulder and said, "Come on, pop, you're holding up the line. Pay the lady and let's get on with it."

"I don't have any more money," he replied. As he turned to face the man behind him, I saw his face for the first time. He had enormous bushy white eyebrows that seemed out of place on his emaciated face, but complemented the thin white moustache on his upper lip. "I've been buying insulin here for years. Always it has been the same price. Now it's four dollars more. My wife"—he threw up his hands in despair—"must have it." He turned back to the clerk.

The lady in front of me grew more agitated. The dozen or so people behind me began craning their necks to see what was holding up the line. Suddenly I stepped out of line, reached into my pocket, withdrew my wallet, and handed five dollars to the old man. "Merry Christmas," I said.

He hesitated a moment, then his blue eyes grew moist as he took the money. "God bless you, my son."

I turned and walked back into the store aisles. I counted the money I had remaining in my wallet— four dollars. I replaced the box of candy on the shelf and got back into line to pay for the novel. The line moved slowly, but at last I made my purchase.

Snow was falling in soft white feathery flakes as I walked up the hill toward our apartment. The lights from the city reflected from the clouds above and gave a glow to my surroundings that matched the glow I felt inside. I turned in our driveway and saw an envelope stuck in our screen door. I removed it and found written on the front of the envelope simply, "Matthew 25:40."

I opened the door, stepped inside, and turned on the light. I ripped open the end of the envelope and withdrew a hundred-dollar bill. There was no other message. With wonder I folded the envelope and stuffed it in my pocket as I heard my wife drive in. She brought in her sack of purchases and shooed me out of our apartment while she did her wrapping.

It was only after I had driven to the department store and purchased the winter coat for my wife that I took time to get out my Bible and read the scripture written on the envelope: "Verily I say unto you, Inasmuch as ye have done it unto one of the least of these my brethren, ye have done it unto me."

To this day I have no idea who blessed our lives that Christmas.

8

Harold Angel

I first met Harold Peterson in the summer of 1965. Because I taught school I always worked a summer job. I had been hired to help run a boys' camp, and Harold was the handyman. At first glance Harold wasn't very impressive. Nearly seventy years of age, he was barely five feet tall and walked with the gait of a man who has spent considerable time in the saddle. I approached him as he was replacing a broken post in the corral. "Hi, you must be Harold."

"Yup," was his total reply. He was wearing a red and black plaid shirt stuffed into a pair of ancient coveralls. He had covered his sparse white hair with a denim cap bearing the logo of a local feed store. His beard was stuffed into the top of the coveralls.

"Looks as if you've done this a time or two."

"Yup."

"Anything I can do to help?"

"Nope." Harold apparently wasn't much for words. But his gnarled old hands fit the new corral pole in place and lashed it securely. I stood watching, thumbs in my belt. When Harold finished, he picked up his tools, threw them in the back of a rusty green Chevrolet pickup, tipped his hat to me, and drove off. I returned to the lodge where we were giving our camp counselors some last-minute instructions before the campers arrived.

After lunch I wandered into the kitchen and talked with the cooks. "Who can fill me in a little on Harold?" All three cooks stopped at once and turned in unison.

"He's the meanest old man I ever met," said the first. "I've never heard him say a good word about anyone."

"Oh, he used to be nicer, when his wife was alive. But since she died, he's been real hard to get close to," said the second.

"Close to!" exclaimed the third. "I don't think you'd want to get close to him. I don't know why they hire him. He scares the campers—not to mention the counselors—and nothing anyone does is done right, according to Harold. He's just trouble." The pitch, tempo, and volume had increased during this disclosure.

I backed out of the kitchen with a little better picture of Harold. I avoided him the rest of the day, which wasn't difficult, since we had over a hundred campers checking in and I had to assign them their cabins and introduce them to their counselors. After dinner, however, when I was walking around camp making sure everybody was where he was supposed to be, I saw Harold limping toward his old green pickup truck. "Where ya going, Harold?"

He barely acknowledged my question, but I heard him growl, "Home." With that he pulled himself into the cab of his truck, turned the key, and coaxed the engine into life. With a spray of dirt and gravel he drove off.

The next morning at sunup I heard his truck pull into the parking lot. Harold had returned. That day I tried a few times to start a conversation with him, but he growled only single words in reply. At sunset he climbed into his truck and away he went.

For six weeks the routine never varied. Harold arrived at sunup, worked all day, and drove down the canyon at sunset. Then came the breakthrough. One morning Harold showed up at camp and loaded some pieces of chain into the back of his truck. "Where are you headed, Harold?" I asked.

Harold responded with the longest reply he had given me in six weeks. "I'm goin' to get some poles for the corral." He started to climb into his truck.

"Need any help?" I asked.

Harold considered my offer, turned slowly, and looked at me. I was prepared for him to refuse, but suddenly he said, "Climb in." We rattled down the dirt and gravel trail to the paved road and turned west for about five miles. Abruptly Harold wrenched the wheel and we bucked down another dirt trail for a mile or so. Harold had not said a word during the entire trip. He stopped the truck in a stand of lodge-pole pine. We climbed out of the truck. Harold handed me a double-bitted axe. "We need twenty-four of them," he said, motioning toward the pines with his hand.

I walked toward a likely pine tree and prepared to strike it with my axe. "Not that one," said Harold, shaking his head in disbelief at my stupidity. "Only the ones that's marked." I looked where he pointed and saw plastic strips attached to a number of the trees. Face burning, I walked to one of those trees and began to swing the axe. As I took my fourth swing Harold yelled, "Timber!" and I turned to see a pine tree falling to the ground.

By noon I'd cut down six trees; Harold had cut down eighteen. We loaded the trees onto his truck with the tops sticking out over the cab and the bases barely missing the ground. The chains secured them to the rusty old Chevrolet. We climbed back into the cab. Harold turned to me, and for the first time in six weeks he smiled briefly and began the conversation. "You're the first one of them guys ever offered to help."

We drove back to camp and unloaded the corral poles. Before Harold left for home that evening we replaced the worn and broken poles. As he climbed into his truck he gave me half a wave and said, "Thanks." Down the road went Harold.

The following Saturday I was driving to Salt Lake to pick up supplies. As I was traveling down the canyon road, I spotted Harold's beat-up old truck ahead of me. I followed him for several miles until he pulled off the road onto a gravel path leading to a small clapboard house. I now knew where Harold lived.

By the end of the summer Harold and I reached the point where we carried on polite conversation, although most of Harold's contribution still consisted of single words. The rest of the camp continued to be terrified of this gruff old Munchkin. When the last camper was gone and my staff had said their farewells, I took a final tour of the camp before leaving. I found Harold draining the water lines that led to the camp from our storage tank. "Thanks for everything, Harold. I guess I'll be going. I'll see you next summer."

Harold just knelt by the water line and without looking up said, "Yup." I walked through the aspen trees to my car and looked back, but Harold hadn't moved. I climbed into my car and drove down the canyon.

I did not think of Harold again until a few months later when I was doing some last-minute Christmas shopping. I spied a display of pocketknives and saw one identical to Harold's. In my mind I saw him slipping it out of his pocket a hundred times a day to cut or trim something or other. I also knew that the tip of the blade had broken off. At that moment I decided that Harold needed a new pocketknife and that it was worth the hour-long drive to his house.

Christmas vacation made it possible for me to drive to several friends' houses on Christmas Eve and deliver gifts to them. I finished by early afternoon and started out of the city to Harold's house. The drive up Parley's Canyon took me into a winter wonderland of snow-covered mountains and icy air. At last I reached Harold's house. The gravel approach had not been cleared of snow, so I parked on the paved road and broke a trail to his front door. I knocked. There was no answer. I knocked again. Still no answer. I put Harold's gift-wrapped knife between the screen door and front door and started back toward my car. The air was thick with the aroma of burning pine, and I noticed a thin column of smoke coming from Harold's chimney.

Just as I started to enter the car I saw movement at the window. Harold was beckoning me back to his house. I plowed back to his door, retrieved his gift, and opened the door to Harold's home. There he sat in a wood-backed chair by the window. His right leg was in a cast from foot to mid-thigh. "Howdy," he said.

I took my coat off and hung it on a wooden peg at the side of the door. "Harold, what happened?"

"Dang knee just gave out on me. It slowed me up some." Further questioning determined that he had been cutting firewood and a tree had landed on his knee. "I've been cutting wood for sixty years and I never had trouble like this before." He had been in the cast for the past three weeks. "I'm kinda glad you showed up. I need some help gettin' some things taken care of." It was the longest conversation Harold had ever initiated.

Harold grabbed a pair of crutches and hauled himself to his feet. Slowly he swung himself across his kitchen and opened the back door. I followed him into his workshop. It felt as if I were entering Santa's workshop. Across the room six rocking horses stared at me with expressionless eyes. A dozen dollhouses, each painted differently, rested on shelves. Children-sized tables and chairs, cupboards, and desks filled the room. "I need your help gettin' these delivered," Harold said.

I examined the handiwork. Carefully assembled, sanded, and painted, they were works of art. "These are beautiful. Did you make them?"

Harold slowly nodded his head. "An old man don't have much to do when he's all alone." He paused; then, as if more justification were needed, he said, "It's been a tough year for some of the families in town. I just figured I'd make a few things for some of the kids." He paused again. "Can you help?"

Who could refuse an invitation like that. At his direction I loaded a table, chairs, dollhouse, and rocking horse into his old green truck. Harold painfully loaded himself into the passenger's side. "We got to be careful, we can't get caught." It was barely dark as I cranked the engine until it finally caught and we broke through the snowdrift onto the road. Harold guided me down a long, snow-packed dirt road on the outskirts of town. At last he told me to stop. "Just around the bend is their house. You gotta carry the stuff from here so they can't see you. Be careful and be quiet. Just leave it on the front porch and get back here."

The rocking horse was the first item. I threw my arms around it and slipped and slid on the snow as I delivered it to the house. As I rounded the corner of the road, I saw the house for the first time. It was a small one-story home covered with white clapboard siding. Here and there a piece of siding had fallen off. An ancient Ford truck with its right rear fender rusted through sat halfway in a shed that leaned precariously to the east. A porch ran the width of the house. The steps to the porch were broken and a number of floorboards were missing. I silently placed the rocking horse on the porch. Light streamed from two windows on the east end of the porch. I carried each item to the front porch and avoided the lighted windows. When I had delivered everything, I got back into the cab of the truck. "So far so good," said Harold. "But we got more to do."

A half dozen more times we returned to Harold's workshed to fill the truck with his handiwork and deliver it to similarly modest homes. It was nearly midnight when we finished. I parked the truck and helped Harold back into his home.

"Looks like you've done that a time or two," I said.

"Yup."

I turned to go, with a special warm feeling inside. "You can't tell anybody, you know," said Harold. "It's just our secret. I don't want to ruin my reputation."

"You're a fraud, Harold," I said, smiling.

"Yup." He handed me my coat. "Merry Christmas. Drive careful."

Warmed by an inner glow, I drove out of that cold mountain valley back to the city.

9

*Blessed Be
the Poor*

"It's a rip-off!"

Dave was not known for his tact on or off the football field. At six feet and 265 pounds, he was usually able to convince others to share his point of view. He and I were walking toward my car in the faculty parking lot. Sandy, a diminutive cheerleader, ran to catch us.

The three of us were on our way to visit a family who had applied for Sub-for-Santa help. From Dave's comments, I believed he considered himself an investigative reporter who would blow the lid off a major scam. As faculty advisor, I wasn't sure why I had been so unlucky as to have been assigned this macho football player to accompany us on our visit. The high school where I taught had a long-standing tradition of participating in the Sub-for-Santa program. The names of families in need were provided by a county social service agency. We developed the habit of sending a faculty advisor with two members of the student council to visit the homes, meet the family, and fill out a Christmas want list.

"I tell you it's a rip-off!" exclaimed Dave again as we pulled out of the parking lot in my ancient Toyota. "These people have just found a way to get a free ride at Christmastime. They really aren't that bad off. Nobody in our town is really that poor."

Sandy sat in the front seat and Dave sprawled over most of the backseat. He kept up his verbal criticism as we drove from our high school, perched on the affluent east bench of our community, west to our destination. At length we reached the address we had been given. It was the first week of December, and light snow swirled around us as we climbed out of the car. We crunched through the gravel driveway, avoided an iced-over puddle, and climbed the steps to the front porch.

A wooden porch ran the length of the front of the house. As we passed by the front window, I noticed the glass had been replaced with a cardboard refrigerator box. The wind gusted against the cardboard and one corner pushed in, allowing snow to blow into the house. We knocked on the door. At length it was opened by a woman dressed in a nondescript gray dress. Her left arm was in a cast. She held a baby against her with her right arm. "Yes?" she questioned. I could see her breath in the coldness of her front room.

"We're from the high school," I said. "We've come to talk about what your children want for Christmas."

"Please come in." The three of us entered the front room of her home. A small child, perhaps three years of age, was wrapped in a blanket and sitting on the floor pushing a block of wood back and forth. The snow had blown in past the cardboard and left a small, unmelting drift in one front corner of the room. There was not one stick of furniture to be seen. "Come into the kitchen. We can be more comfortable in there." She led us through a doorway.

The kitchen had an old wooden table and two unmatched chairs. "Have a seat."

I sat. I looked around the kitchen. There were no doors on the cupboards, and I could see a single can of tomato soup on one shelf. The others were empty. Dave and Sandy stood uncomfortably in one corner. Dressed in his five-hundred-dollar, down-filled parka, Dave looked strangely out of place in these sparse surroundings. The child in the front room cried for his mother. Our hostess excused herself to look after her son. Sandy took advantage of her absence to open the refrigerator. A solitary carton of milk was inside. No light came on. In fact there were no lights on in the house, even though the snow storm had made the day dark. There was no fear of the milk spoiling, however, since the house was as cold as a refrigerator.

Our hostess returned. As she and I talked, Sandy and Dave walked back into the front room. From the corner of my eye I watched them open a door and look into a bedroom. "Tell me the names of your children and their ages," I prompted.

"Mandy—she's the oldest—she's eight, almost nine. Then there's Bud, he's six. Paula's five; she just started school this year. Mike's just turned three, and Ginger here's seven months old. She was born just after her father died."

"I'm sorry," I said. "What happened?"

"He was a truck driver and his rig rolled over in a

windstorm out near Wendover." The conversation continued, and I found out she married during her junior year in high school. When her husband died, the funeral expenses had used up all of their savings. She had no job skills to speak of but finally found employment as an orderly at the local hospital. She worked the midnight shift so she could be home with her children. Three weeks before, she had slipped on a wet floor at the hospital and fractured her elbow. The hospital paid the medical expenses. She was determined to make it on her own but felt the need to ask for help for her children for Christmas.

Sandy and Dave entered the kitchen. Dave blurted out, "It sure is cold in here."

"We got a little behind on our payments and the gas was turned off." There was a resigned shrug of her shoulders. "Electricity got cut off, too. But I'll be out of the cast in three more weeks and then things will get better."

"I'd like to make a list of what your children want for Christmas," I said. "Let's start with Mandy. What does she want for Christmas?"

Her head dropped and her eyes searched the floor. "Well—Mandy—that's a tough one. She wants one of them Barbie dolls and I know they cost a lot. I'm sure she'd understand if she didn't get one."

"What else does she want?" I asked.

"Oh, nothing. She just wants a doll, that's all. The kids, they know there won't be much for Christmas this year."

I continued with Bud, Paula, Mike, and Ginger's requests. For each only a single item was asked. All of the items together couldn't have cost more than thirty dollars. After some gentle prompting, I wrote down clothing and shoe sizes. "Anything else?"

"No . . . well, maybe a Christmas tree. It wouldn't have to be big, and it wouldn't need no ornaments or lights. 'Course the power don't work anyway, so we don't need no lights. But a tree would be nice."

I closed my notebook and we walked to the porch. It seemed slightly warmer outside than in. I told her we would be in touch, and we walked down the gravel to my car. As before, Dave climbed into the backseat and Sandy into the front seat. As I put the key in the ignition I felt the car shaking. I looked into the rearview mirror and saw Dave crying in the backseat. His convulsive sobs were shaking the car. Sandy said quietly, "We're going to help those people. We are. We are."

The next morning at school Sub-for-Santa families were assigned to departments. I requested that *our* family be given to the science department, since I taught biology. Dave and Sandy began whipping up enthusiasm among our students. I had extracted a promise from them that they would not reveal the name or location of our family. In order to preserve the privacy of the family and avoid, as much as possible, any embarrassment, we were always assigned families outside our school area.

Assigning Sub-for-Santa families to different departments of the school provided possibilities for competition between the departments. Dave demanded that we challenge the English department to raise more money than the science department. The English department had more teachers than any other department in the school, since every student had to enroll in an English class each year. The odds were in their favor. Soon I saw the method in Dave's plan. Due to their sheer numbers, the English classes would contribute more money than any other department. That meant we had to raise more money to meet the challenge. Our four first-period science classes had to raise more money than seven first-period English classes.

It worked! The competition was limited to two weeks. By the end of the first week we were neck and neck with the English department, but enthusiasm was waning. Dave and Sandy asked if they could speak to our first-period classes. They entered my biology class and thumbtacked a poster to the front bulletin board. On the poster Sandy had neatly lettered the needs of our family. The list began with the broken front window, continued through lack of electricity and heat, described the lack of food and furniture, and ended with the list of five Christmas gifts that had been requested. Sandy read the list to the class. There appeared to be polite interest. Suddenly Dave jumped to his feet.

"You guys aren't listening!" he bellowed. "Man, I've been there, and these people are hurting! We need to help them for Christmas. Don't just sit there, they need help!" He began to describe graphically what he had seen on his visit to their home. He completed his discourse by telling the students that while I was talking to the lady of the house, he and Sandy had gone into the bedrooms. "There aren't any clothes in the closets, and they sleep on mattresses on the floor!"

As Dave talked, the polite interest turned into intense interest. When tears started streaming down his cheeks, it turned into awe. "My dad runs a glass company," volunteered Peaches from her third-row seat. "I'll bet he'd give us a real good deal on a window." The floodgates opened. Suddenly someone remembered a couch his family was getting rid of, someone else remembered an extra bed, and on and on.

After Dave's emotional plea, it was no contest. We beat the English department by over two hundred dollars. Clothing, furniture, and toys continued to flow in. "Peaches," I asked, "did you talk to your father about a window?" She nodded. "How much will it cost us?"

Peaches smiled. "Dave gave me the address. Dad's already put it in. It's his donation to Sub-for-Santa. It won't cost us anything."

My classroom was filling fast. I now had six beds, a couch and matching chair, three rolls of carpet, and seven or eight boxes of canned food crammed into an already overcrowded classroom. "When are we going to deliver it?" asked Sandy. It was Monday of the last week before Christmas vacation. Christmas was on Friday, and we were scheduled to get out of school Wednesday afternoon at one o'clock.

"Let's take everything as soon as we're released for vacation," I answered. "Dave has a pickup truck and I can borrow one. We can probably take everything down in three or four loads."

"Dave and I have an idea," said Sandy. "We thought maybe we ought to deliver on Christmas Eve. Perhaps Santa and his two elves could deliver that night. That will give us time to finish the Christmas tree."

In the flurry of holiday preparations, I had forgotten the request for a Christmas tree. We had taken the donated money and paid the back utility bills. A substantial reserve had been left with the gas, electricity, and water companies. We had shopped for new clothing and the gift requests. We had wrapped and tagged the gifts. We had stuffed all of these goodies into my classroom. But I had forgotten the Christmas tree.

"Dave and I bought the tree. It was kind of our special gift to our family. We need some help, though, figuring out how to keep the decorations on while we drive from here to their house. Can we go Christmas Eve? Please."

I explained our request to the principal, a kind and caring man. At first he said he would arrange for a custodian to be at the school to let us in, but in the end said it would be easier if he were there to help. When we were excused for Christmas vacation, Dave brought the tree into my room. With the help of most of my class, we glued ornament hangers into ornaments and twisted them around branches with needle-nose pliers. As strings of lights were clipped to branches, a twist tie was added to hold each light securely. Tinsel was also twist-tied to branches. A star was wired securely to the top of the tree. We were ready.

At 10:00 P.M. Christmas Eve, Dave, Sandy, the principal, and I met at the school. Each of us had a pickup truck. We loaded furniture, food, gifts, and the tree into the trucks. It took us over an hour. When everything had been loaded, I went back into the school and put on my Santa Claus outfit. As I emerged and headed for my pickup truck, much to my amazement I discovered not only Dave and Sandy in elf outfits, but the principal as well. "I'm not being left out of this," he said.

The procession through town went slowly. Despite our best efforts, the ornaments on the Christmas tree bounced around in the wind. It was nearly midnight when we arrived at our destination. We

backed the four pickup trucks onto the front lawn. I
walked onto the front porch, noticed the new window, and tried the front door. It opened to reveal the
bare front room. At least it was a warm front room. I
tried the light switch and a ceiling light came on.
Immediately my elves unloaded a roll of carpeting,
carried it through the front door, and unrolled it on
the floor. It fit! Sandy saw the amazed look on my
face. "We came down and measured . . . Santa."

At that moment bedroom doors popped open and
amazed faces appeared. The couch was carried
through the front door and deposited. "Have a seat,
Santa," said my biggest elf.

I sat down on the couch and motioned to the
eldest child. "Come here, Mandy." With eyes as big as
saucers she crossed the room and sat on my knee.

"I didn't think you were coming. Mom said you
weren't coming this year."

I smiled at this innocent face, gave her a hug, and
asked, "What do you want for Christmas, Mandy?"
In the background I watched chairs, tables, and beds
march in through the door and go to the appropriate
rooms while I took each of the children on my knee
and talked to them.

"Santa, we need your help," said Sandy elf. My
other two elves had brought the Christmas tree to the
front porch. The four of us carefully pressed against
branches so the ornaments made it through the door.
We stood it in a corner and I plugged in the lights.
Suddenly there was a hush in the room. The children
sat on the floor and looked at the tree. "It's beautiful!
The most beautiful tree we've ever had," exclaimed
the mother of our family.

While Dave elf hauled in the wrapped packages,
the other two brought in food and stocked the shelves

in the kitchen. I handed gifts to each of the children as I called out their names, and made them promise not to open them until morning. We turned to go. "Merry Christmas," we called out.

Our hostess handed the baby to Mandy. She hugged each of the elves, turned to me, and as she hugged me said, "Thank you, Santa. We thought you weren't coming. How can we ever repay you?"

I looked at the five glitter-eyed children and said, "You already have."

I often read in newspapers of teenagers who get into trouble. It seems as if there is a conspiracy to prove the younger generation is beyond hope. If you had shared with me that memorable Christmas Eve, you would know why it is easy for me to see great hope for the future in the lives of the youth of today. "Merry Christmas," and "God bless us . . . everyone."

10

Angela Ann

Charlie and I had not seen each other since we graduated from college. He took a job that required a move to Phoenix, Arizona. I became a teacher in Bountiful, Utah. We were fast friends in school, and when we discovered Charlie was moving, we went to dinner and vowed to keep in touch. Ten years passed without a letter or a phone call from either of us. Then the phone rang. Charlie had moved back to Salt Lake.

The following Saturday I met him at his office for lunch. We blamed each other for not calling or writing, smiled, and sat down in his office to catch up on the past decade. Charlie's office was tastefully decorated in dark wood and turquoise. On his desk was a framed picture of his wife, Nell, and their twin sons. The only item that seemed out of place was a small stuffed teddy bear sitting on his bookshelf. "Your security blanket?" I joked.

Charlie was silent for a moment, then said, "This is Telly." He removed the bear from the shelf. I could see it had only one eye. One ear had been chewed into oblivion. "Let's go to lunch and I'll tell you about him." There was a hushed reverence in his voice, and I thought his eyes were going to overflow. We went to a restaurant close by, and while we ate Charlie told me this story.

About a week before Christmas, Charlie's next-door neighbors Paul and Kathy Walker received a phone call informing them of Paul's brother's untimely death. They quickly made arrangements, packed their three children into the car, and headed for Los Angeles to attend the funeral. While they were gone their water heater sprang a leak. They had a sunken family room, which turned into a shallow swimming pool. As the water reached the electrical outlets, circuit breakers blew and the house was plunged into darkness. The refrigerator quit working. The whole house was flooded.

The funeral was on December 23. Following the funeral the Walkers drove all night back to Arizona. They arrived early on the morning of Christmas Eve. Paul drove into the driveway, grabbed a suitcase, and approached the back door. He saw water on the porch as he tried to open the door. It resisted his efforts. Finally putting his shoulder against the door, he pushed it open and a torrent of water rushed out.

Charlie became aware of the problem when he heard his doorbell ring. Sleepily he climbed out of bed and made his way to the door. Kathy Walker stood there sobbing. "We've been flooded," she moaned. "Everything's ruined."

Charlie and Nell dressed quickly and waded in to help assess the damage. Couches and overstuffed chairs were waterlogged. The food in the refrigerator was spoiled. Soaked sheetrock was disintegrating. Swimming in the family room was the Christmas tree and the family's Christmas gifts.

Charlie began waking up the neighborhood. The main valve to the water line was located and shut off. Equipment was brought and water pumped out of the house. By noon all of the furniture had been carried out of the house and spread around the yard to see which might be salvaged and which would be carried off to the dump. It was clear that little could be saved.

Among those who showed up to help was the Blair family, who lived in the only basement apartment in the neighborhood. Ralph had been born in 1914 and dropped out of school at age sixteen during the Depression. Ruth was two years younger. When they met in 1956 neither had married nor had any thoughts of marriage. However, they found companionship with each other, fell in love, and married six months later. Two years later Angela Ann was born. She was to be their only child.

Angela Ann was a Down's syndrome child. The doctors gave her five years to live. Now at fourteen she was a miracle child. At first she had been Angela, which she shortened to Gela, and finally she called herself Jelly. "I, Jelly Blair," she proudly announced. Jelly's constant companion was a one-eyed teddy bear. "Telly Blair," she called him. He often hung by his ear from her mouth. She had come with her parents to help the Walkers.

The Walkers' insurance agent arrived and began assessing the damage. While he had Paul and Kathy occupied, Charlie invited the neighbors into his house. "It seems to me," he began, "we ought to do something to make the Walkers' Christmas a little happier. I don't know what they'd planned, but I'm pretty sure all of their presents are ruined." Heads nodded in agreement. "I do know we've gotten more for our twins than they really need, and I think we'd be willing to share with our neighbors."

Charlie paused in his narrative. "I wasn't sure Nell and our boys would agree, but they were really more enthusiastic than I was. They rushed into our front room and brought back wrapped presents to donate to the Walkers."

He continued with his story. "It really ought to be anonymous," said Ruth Blair quietly from the corner. "I mean, some of us may have more to share than others. I think no one ought to know what anyone else has given." Again heads nodded in agreement.

"I'll pull the car out of the garage," said Charlie, "and anything anyone wants to donate can be put in there. I'll make sure everything gets delivered tonight." The crowd began to disperse.

Charlie walked over to the Walkers' house. Their insurance agent was just leaving. "They're going to put us up in a rented house while the repairs go on," said Kathy. "It's surely going to be a mess to straighten out." Her eyes filled with tears as she surveyed the ruined furniture in their yard.

Within an hour, the Walkers began moving clothing and food to the rental house a half dozen blocks away. Charlie and other neighbors pitched in to help. Kathy stayed at their home and handed out salvaged items to helpers who filled their cars and drove to the rental house where Paul directed the unloading efforts. By sunset the Walkers at least had a place to stay.

After depositing the last load, Charlie drove into his driveway. The lights from his car lit up the pile of presents in his garage. Dozens of brightly wrapped gifts were stacked on the floor. To one side he could see a fully decorated Christmas tree. Nell met him at the door. "It's been coming all afternoon. It seems everybody just watches to make sure there's no one else in the garage and then here they come with an armful of packages. Dan Grange brought the Christmas tree. They had two, one in the living room and one in their family room, and thought Paul and Kathy ought to have one."

"How do we get it all delivered?" asked Charlie.

"Well, I've been busy, too. The Granges invited the Walkers to dinner tonight. They ought to be arriving any minute. I've got two pickup trucks coming to move everything while they're eating." As Nell spoke, the Walkers' familiar station wagon arrived at the Granges' home. Within minutes the two trucks arrived at Charlie's. Quickly the Christmas tree was loaded, followed by the colorful gifts.

As Charlie was loading the last few presents into his car, his hand touched a small, furry creature. He lifted it from the pile of gifts and stared at a one-eyed, ragged bear.

Charlie paused again in his narrative. "That's the story. That's where I got Telly."

"But what about the gifts?" I queried. "What happened?"

"The other gifts were delivered. We drove the trucks slowly, very slowly, to their rental house. The Christmas tree looked a little windblown, but was still presentable. We unloaded everything and slipped away before the Walkers returned. Everything went as planned. All of us felt the Christmas spirit. I'm sure the Walkers had a nice Christmas. Within a month everything was repaired and they were back in their own home."

Charlie's eyes grew misty. "But I just couldn't leave Telly. The rest of us gave of our surplus. Jelly gave the widow's mite. I knew how Jelly loved that bear. I thought about returning it to her. But I couldn't ruin it for Jelly. Instead I keep it on my shelf to remind me . . ." Charlie's voice trailed off.

"Remind you of what?" I asked softly.

"Of giving of yourself. That's what Christmas is all about, isn't it?"

We returned to Charlie's office.

The one-eyed, ear-chewed bear smiled silently at us from its place of honor.

11

Have Faith,
My Son

I was serving my fourth Christmas as a bishop for The Church of Jesus Christ of Latter-day Saints, and was interviewing one of the young women in the ward. Her sixteenth birthday had been December 11, and I was now conducting a birthday interview the following Sunday. All during our talk she stared at the floor. "What's wrong, Tina?" I asked.

She raised her eyes to meet mine, and I saw tears rolling down her cheeks. "Christmas is just a week away and our family doesn't have anything."

Although I'm sure I tried to hide my surprise, it must have been obvious. "I had no idea. Your family seems so . . . so . . ."

"So rich!" she said bitterly. "It's all just show. Haven't you noticed no one is ever invited into our house?"

I remembered the few times I had visited. Often I

had sensed someone was at home, although no one answered the door. The only time I had spoken with anyone at their home was when Tina's father talked to me in their front yard. They had lived in the ward for almost a year and I had never been inside their home.

"I had no idea," I repeated, feeling guilty.

"Dad would be furious with me if he knew I was telling you this. Nobody's ever invited in because everything in our house is so old. The couch has holes in it. The rug in the front room's all covered with stains. We don't even have a table in the kitchen. We just sit on the floor and eat." The tears were coming faster.

"Why didn't you tell me?"

"Dad and Mom are so proud," she said bitterly. "They won't tell anyone. They sure won't ask for help."

I was still dumbfounded. "You all dress so neatly," was the only thing I could think of to say.

"Grandma sends us clothes. I don't know where she gets them. She works for a distribution center or something. Anyway, we get clothes all the time from Grandma." I could tell the interview was over as Tina rose and moved toward the door. "Don't tell Mom or Dad . . . please!"

After she left I sat at my desk and thought about what could be done to help. The youth of the ward had already participated in a Sub-for-Santa project for a family in another ward in our area. I had turned to the more affluent members of the ward for financial help for two other families who were struggling. I just didn't know where I could turn to raise more funds. I was reluctant to use Church funds for Christmas presents.

I bowed my head and asked, "Father, where do I go? How do I help these proud people?"

The Spirit whispered, "Have faith, my son. Determine their needs."

At times I am slow to listen, and I prayed, "But Father, where do I go?"

"Have faith."

I finished my prayer, left the chapel, and walked home. The night was clear, the air cold and crisp. Each breath created a cloud. *How do I help them?* I thought. *How do I determine their needs? How do I find out what the children want for Christmas when I can't even get through the front door?*

"Have faith," the Spirit whispered.

The next afternoon I came home from work and found Tina's younger sister, Joanie, playing with my daughter. Although my daughter Sherri often brought friends home, Joanie had never been in our home before. When dinner was ready, Sherri said good-bye to her friend and came to the dinner table.

"Listen," said the Spirit.

"Guess what," said Sherri. "Joanie and I want nearly the same things for Christmas."

"Oh, really!" I exclaimed. "How do you know that?"

"We were talking. I know everything she wants and her brother wants, and her sisters want. I know everything her whole family wants for Christmas."

"Listen," said the Spirit.

I reached for a pad of paper. "Why don't you tell me what they want, Sherri. I'm really interested."

Sherri recited a Christmas list for Joanie followed by one for Tina, Brad, and Melissa. I carefully wrote the list down. After the children were in bed my wife found me sitting on the edge of our bed mulling over the list. "How come you're so interested in that Christmas list?" she asked.

"Oh, just wondering how much it would cost to buy everything on this list."

"Let me look at it," she said. Pen in hand, she began jotting figures next to the items. "It looks like nearly eight hundred dollars."

I whistled. "That much. Wow!" As I tossed and turned in bed that night, I wondered where I could find that much money.

"Have faith," the Spirit whispered.

I spent the rest of the week wondering who I could approach to try to raise that much money. By the next Sunday, the last one before Christmas, I had contacted all of the people on my list. I had raised just over one hundred dollars.

Following our scheduled meetings, I became involved in the year-end process of tithing settlement. It was after ten o'clock before the last family had left the church. I turned out the light in my office and walked around the church to make sure the doors were locked. When I finished I sat down on a bench in the chapel and said, "Well, three more days to Christmas and seven hundred dollars to find."

"Have faith," whispered the Spirit. A great feeling of peace and calm came over me. "You have done your part, all will be well."

I rose and walked out of the church. I noticed a car parked next to mine, and as I approached I could see someone behind the wheel. When I reached my car the door of the other car opened and its occupant stepped out. "Bishop."

"Yes. I'm sorry, I don't know who you are."

"It doesn't matter. I need your help. My company has done extremely well this year. I have been richly blessed, and I have the feeling you could use a small contribution. Would you make certain this is put to good use?" He handed me an envelope and quickly got back in his car.

"Certainly," I said, "but please tell me who you are."

"It doesn't matter." He paused, then said, "Merry Christmas." He started his car and drove carefully from the snow-covered parking lot.

I sat down in my car and turned on the light. Carefully I opened the envelope. Inside were eight one-hundred-dollar bills. I quickly started my car and drove out of the parking lot. The other car and its occupant were nowhere to be seen.

I enlisted my wife's help in shopping the next afternoon and evening. When all purchases were paid for we had spent $896. The gifts were anonymously and lovingly delivered.

12

Amy's Song

There are advantages and disadvantages to living in a small town. One advantage is that everyone knows everyone else. One disadvantage is that everyone knows everyone else. Everyone knew Amy Williams, only child. She had been born seventeen years ago crippled in body if not in spirit. No one expected her to live, but she had. Everyone knew Amy Williams. Her hunched back and twisted spine were recognizable at a distance. Here she sat outside the choral room door, agonizing.

What am I doing here? she thought to herself. *I'll never be chosen for a part.*

One advantage to small towns is that they develop traditions. A Christmas tradition in Marysvale was the annual pageant performed in the school auditorium. It had been performed for so many years that no one could remember when it had begun or even who had written it. But it had become the focal point of the Christmas season for many of the townspeople.

I don't want to go through the rejection again, thought Amy. *I try not to care, but I do. I don't want to be hurt anymore.*

More people tried out each year for parts in the pageant than could possibly be used. Young children hoped to be shepherd boys, older ones the shepherds or the Wise Men. Those who sang hoped to be part of the angelic choir; a chosen few the innkeeper, the angel of the Lord, Joseph, Mary. Many were turned away, for the stage in the old schoolhouse was small. The choir was a dozen or so voices. There was room for only a half dozen shepherds and three wise men.

Mr. Simons will never choose me for a part. I just don't fit. But at least I don't have to audition in front of Mrs. Prendergast, mused Amy.

Mrs. Prendergast had been the music teacher at Marysvale High School for over thirty years. She had cast, coached, directed, and accompanied the pageant all those years. When Amy had been a freshman, three years ago, she had tried out for the pageant. Mrs. Prendergast had taken one look at Amy's misshapen body and in her dragon voice said, "Child, you just don't fit. I don't remember anywhere in the script where it calls for a crippled girl. Everyone would stare at you and that would make you uncomfortable. It would make them uncomfortable, too."

Without singing a single note, Amy had been thrust back through the choral room door. She shuffled home hurt and humiliated and vowed never to try out again. Then . . . Mrs. Prendergast retired.

This year they had a new choral teacher, Mr. Simons. He was the opposite of Mrs. Prendergast. She had ruled with fear and force. He led with love and compassion. Amy liked him from the first. He demanded perfection, but understood when it was not reached. He coached and corrected with kindness. And he sang himself with such power. It was he who had asked Amy to see him after class and had suggested she audition for the pageant.

I ought to leave now and avoid the pain. There's no place for a girl like me in the pageant. I don't want to be rejected again. Still . . . Mr. Simons asked me to try out. I owe it to him. But he'll never choose me. I'm going to leave before it's my turn.

As Amy struggled to her feet, the door was pushed open and Mr. Simons called out, "Amy, you're next." He sat at the piano, waiting to accompany her. When she finished singing, Mr. Simons said, "Thank you, Amy. The list will be posted tomorrow."

She struggled all night long. Back and forth her mind went between the reality of knowing she didn't fit and the great need to be accepted. By morning she had a knot in the pit of her stomach and could not bring herself to look at the list on the choral room door. But as her third-period music class approached, she knew that avoiding it would not change the outcome. Timidly, fearfully, she looked at the list. At the bottom of the page was listed the heavenly choir. As she suspected, her name was not among those listed. Rejected again! She turned to enter the class when her eye caught her name posted at the top of the page. She, Amy Williams, had been chosen to sing the only solo part in the whole pageant. She was to be the angel of the Lord. She was to sing to the Christ child, the Son of God. There had to be a mistake. Certainly Mr. Simons would not put her in that part. It was so visible.

"Amy," called Mr. Simons from the piano, "we need to talk about your part after class."

Class seemed to last forever. Finally it ended and she made her way to Mr. Simons's side. "You wanted to talk to me?"

"Amy, I hope this doesn't upset you, but I need to stage your part a little differently this year."

Hidden offstage, she thought.

Mr. Simons continued: "I would like to have a pyramid built, place the other angels on it, and put you at the very top. I know in the past they've put the angel just a bit above the shepherds, but I think the message you sing is the central part of the pageant."

The years of hurt exploded. "You don't want me in the middle of the stage! Won't the way I look ruin the whole thing? You don't want me where everybody will stare at me!"

"Amy, I chose you because you deserve the part. What you think of yourself I cannot change. That is something only you can deal with. I have no problem with you singing this part, and in this pageant the angel of the Lord is center stage. You must come to peace with yourself or you must tell me to choose someone else for the part. It is your decision."

That night Amy made her decision. The rehearsals were exhausting. Her body ached after struggling to the top of the pyramid, but great joy filled her heart.

One advantage to living in a small town is that when there is a community event, everyone attends. And so it was the Sunday before Christmas when the whole town of Marysvale attended the Christmas pageant. Amy Williams, only child, misshapen of body if not of spirit, stood on the top of a silver-white pyramid and sang her heart out to the Christ child . . . and to his brother.

Fear not: for, behold, I bring you good tidings of great joy, which shall be to all people. For unto you is born this day in the city of David a Saviour, which is Christ the Lord.

What Child is this, who, laid to rest,
On Mary's lap is sleeping? . . .

Never had the angel sung more sweetly.

No one had realized how sick Amy really was, I suppose, because they were so used to seeing her broken body. So it was a shock when she died that next Tuesday. Her mother conveyed a last request from Amy to Mr. Simons. Would he please sing at her funeral?

"I've never been in your church . . . it would be very difficult." The excuses continued, but in the end he agreed.

And so that Christmas Eve two of Amy's classmates, two boys from the bass section, helped Mr. Simons from his wheelchair and supported him as he sang for a daughter of God, as she had sung for His Son.

There are advantages to living in a small town.

About the Author

Richard M. Siddoway was raised in Salt Lake City, Utah. He received a bachelor's degree from the University of Utah and a master's degree in instructional systems and learning resources from the same institution. A professional educator for over twenty-five years, he is currently the director of library media services for the Davis County School District. He is a former bishop and now serves as a member of the stake presidency in the Val Verda Stake in Bountiful, Utah. *Twelve Tales of Christmas* is his first published book.

The author and his wife, the former Geri Hendrickson, had six children prior to her untimely death from cancer. He has since remarried the former Janice Spires, and they have a combined family of eight children.